Hurricane Dancers

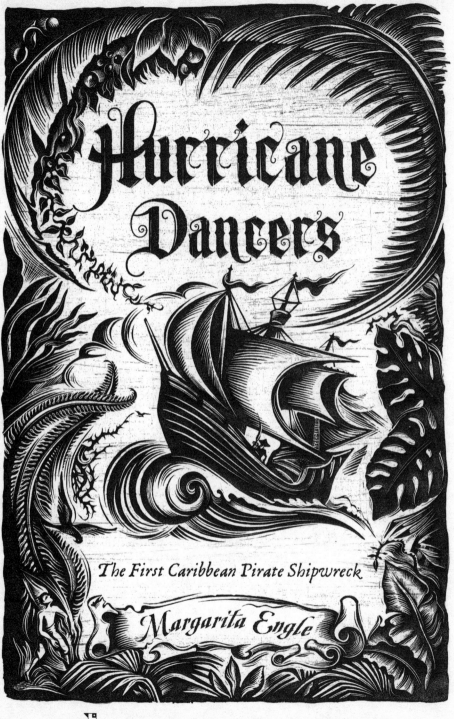

Hurricane Dancers

The First Caribbean Pirate Shipwreck

Margarita Engle

SQUARE FISH

HENRY HOLT AND COMPANY · NEW YORK

In memory of my Cuban Indian ancestors

SQUARE
FISH

An Imprint of Macmillan
175 Fifth Avenue
New York, NY 10010
macteenbooks.com

Square Fish books may be purchased for business or promotional use.
For information on bulk purchases, please contact the Macmillan Corporate and
Premium Sales Department at (800) 221-7945 x 5442 or by e-mail at
specialmarkets@macmillan.com.

Library of Congress Cataloging-in-Publication Data
Engle, Margarita.
Hurricane dancers : the first Caribbean pirate shipwreck / Margarita Engle.
        p.   cm.
Includes bibliographical references.
ISBN 978-1-250-04010-7 (paperback)
1. Shipwrecks—Caribbean Area—Juvenile poetry.   2. Pirates—Caribbean
Area—History—16th century—Juvenile poetry.   3. Indians of the West Indies—
Juvenile poetry.   4. Caribbean Area—Juvenile poetry.   5. Children's poetry,
American.   I. Title.   II. Title: First Caribbean pirate shipwreck.
PS3555.N4254H87 2011   811'.54—dc22   2010011690

Originally published in the United States by Henry Holt and Company
First Square Fish Edition: 2014
Book designed by Liz Herzog
Square Fish logo designed by Filomena Tuosto

1   3   5   7   9   10   8   6   4   2

AR: 6.6 / LEXILE: 1170L

Be not afeard; the isle is full of noises, sounds, and sweet airs, that give delight and hurt not.

Caliban
from *The Tempest*
by William Shakespeare

Bernardino de Talavera was deeply in debt, like so many Spaniards who worked their Indians to death, yet could not prosper. He assembled a group of seventy characters in rags for debts and other unpunished crimes, and together they stole a ship. . . .

Bartolomé de las Casas
Historia de las Indias

CONTENTS

HISTORICAL SETTING

Spanish ships reached the western Caribbean Sea in 1492, searching for Asia and spices. Instead, the explorers found peaceful islanders, and enslaved them.

By 1510, the Bahamas, Hispaniola, Puerto Rico, and Jamaica had been conquered. Only Cuba, the largest Caribbean isle, was still free.

It was a time of hurricanes on an island of hope.

CAST OF CHARACTERS

Quebrado (keh-BRAH-doe): A young ship's slave of Taíno Indian and Spanish ancestry

Bernardino de Talavera
(ber-nar-DEE-no deh tah-lah-VEH-rah): The first pirate of the Caribbean Sea

Alonso de Ojeda
(ah-LON-so de oh-HEH-dah): The pirate's hostage, a brutal conquistador

Naridó (nah-ree-DOE): A young Ciboney Indian fisherman

Caucubú (kow-koo-BOO): The young daughter of a Ciboney chieftain

Caciques (kah-SEE-kehs): Chieftains
Behiques (beh-EE-kehs): Shamans
Ciboney and Taíno Indian tribesmen, women, and children
Spanish sailors
Spirits
Ghosts

Part One

Wild Sea

Quebrado

I listen
to the song
of creaking planks,
the roll and sway
of clouds in sky,
wild music
and thunder,
the groans
of wood,
a mourning moan
as this old ship
remembers
her true self,
her tree self,
rooted
and growing,
alive,
on shore.

Quebrado

One glance is enough to show me
the pirate's mood.

There are days when he treats me
like an invisible wisp of night,
and days when he crushes me
like a cockroach on his table.

I try to slip away
each time I see
his coiled fist,
even though
on a ship
there is no place
to hide.

Quebrado

The sailors call me *el quebrado*,
"the broken one," a child of two
shattered worlds, half islander
and half outsider.

My mother was a *natural*, a "native"
of the island called *cu ba*, "Big Friend,"
home of my first few wild
hurricane seasons.

My father was a man of the sea,
a Spanish army deserter.
When my mother's people
found him on horseback,
starving in the forest,
they fed him, and taught him
how to live like a *natural*.

To become a peaceful Taíno,
he traded his soldier-name
for Gua Iro, "Land Man."
He and my mother

were happy together,
until a plague took the village,
and none were left
but my wandering father,
who roamed far away,
leaving me alone
with his copper-hued horse
in an unnatural village
of bat-winged spirits
and guava-eating ghosts.

Sailors call me a boy
of broken dreams,
but I think of myself
as a place—a strange place
dreamed by the sea,
belonging nowhere,
half floating island
and half
wandering wind.

Quebrado

I survived alone in the ghostly village,
with only my father's abandoned horse
to console me, until a moonlit night
when I was seized by rough seafarers,
wild men who beat me
and taught me how to sail,
and how to lose hope.

I was traded from ship to ship as a slave,
until I ended up in the service
of Bernardino de Talavera,
the pirate captain of this stolen vessel.

The pirate finds me useful
because I know two tongues,
my mother's flutelike Taíno,
and my father's drumlike Spanish.

Together, my two languages
sound like music.

Quebrado

How can a father abandon a son
in such a dangerous world?
Why did he leave me alone
in that village of ghosts
with only his red horse
for company?

What kind of horseman
abandons his steed?

A sorrowful man,
that is the answer.

I have spent all my years
accepting sad truths.

Bernardino de Talavera

I once owned a vast land grant
with hundreds of *naturales*,
Indian slaves who perished
from toil, hunger, and plagues.
Crops withered, mines failed.
All my dreams of wealth vanished.

Soldiers soon gave chase,
trying to send me to debtors' prison,
so I captured this ship and seized
a valuable hostage, Alonso de Ojeda,
Governor of Venezuela,
an immense, jungled province
on the South American mainland,
where he is known
as the most ruthless
conqueror of tribes.

When I heard that Ojeda
had been wounded by a warrior's
frog-poisoned arrow,
I offered help, assuring the Governor

that my ship would gladly carry him
to any port with Spanish doctors.

I offered the illusion of mercy,
and Ojeda was desperate enough
to believe me.

Quebrado

The pirate demands a ransom,
but the hostage insists
he has nothing to give,
so while they argue,
I lean over the creaking ship's
splintered rail,
watching with wonder
as blue dolphins
leap and soar
like winged spirits.

My mother believed dolphins
can change their shape, turning
into men who come ashore
to sing and dance during storms.

If legless creatures
can be transformed,
maybe someday
I will change too.

Bernardino de Talavera

I catch the broken boy,
and it takes only a few quick blows
to convince Ojeda
of my strength.

When the prisoner sees my power
over a slave boy, he understands
that I would show even less mercy
to a grown man.

Knights who have lost
their guns and swords
are remarkably easy
to frighten.

Alonso de Ojeda

All my life, I have been triumphant.
On the isle of Hispaniola, I tricked
a chieftain by offering him a ride on my horse,
then trapping him in handcuffs.
I sent him away in the hold of a ship,
to be sold as a curiosity in Spain,
but a hurricane sank the vessel
while the chief was still shackled.
Expecting rebellion, I slaughtered
his queen and all her people,
to keep them from seeking revenge.

There were days when my sword
killed ten thousand.

Now, all those dead spirits haunt me,
and I am the one on a ship
in chains.

Quebrado

The life of a ship's slave
is hard labor and fists,
or deep water and sharks.

When I sleep, I belong to the land.
In dreams, I work in a field,
planting roots in rich soil.

In dreams, I feel like a spirit of the air,
riding my father's leaping horse.

In dreams, I feel free,
until the sun rises and my eyes open,
and once again I must struggle
beneath the weight
of flapping sails
and heavy ropes.

Quebrado

My mother loved the green parrots
and red macaws that made the sky
above our village look so cheerful.
She always had at least one raucous bird
perched on her shoulder.

As if by magic, the clever birds
learned to speak two languages.
My first words of Taíno and Spanish
were mastered by listening to songs
recited by feathered creatures
of the air.

Now, each time I think of home,
I remember that the world
is big enough to offer more
than sorrow.

Quebrado

The sea is wild today.
The sails look like wings.

Sailors chant tales while they work—
sweet songs about the Island of Mermaids,
and scary ones about the Isle of Giants,
with green jungles where huge women
turn into monsters, clasping sailors
in their talons.

The sea is wild tonight.
The roaring wind
sounds hungry.

Alonso de Ojeda

Shackled to a rotting wall
in the ship's stinking hold,
I feel as helpless as a turtle
flipped on its back,
awaiting the cook's
probing knife.

I clench my fists
and struggle
to fight my way
out of the handcuffs,
while ghosts
gather around me,
watching
and waiting. . . .

Bernardino de Talavera

The hostage begs for mercy,
but I have enough trouble
just trying to figure out
how to steer
the stubborn ship
in this devil wind,
and how to reach land,
and where to await
fair weather.

In a storm, the only decision
that really matters
is direction.

Quebrado

The sky is alive with cloud dragons
and wind spirits.

When a sailor is almost swept overboard,
I wish that I had a gold ring in my ear,
like the one the pirate wears for luck.
His red shirt is meant to ward away
evil winds, and he ties a green cloth
around his head for protection.

The rest of us are dressed in rags,
except for the shackled hostage,
who wears armor and an amulet
with the painted face of a wistful saint.

I wonder if the saint looks so sad
because she knows how many people
Ojeda has killed.

Quebrado

I carry a brass bell
that clangs
with each step,
hoping to soothe
the angry wind
by ringing out
a festive melody.

If only my own
rising fear
of this howling storm
and the pirate's fury
and Ojeda's screams
could be calmed
by a remedy
as simple
as music.

Alonso de Ojeda

I am a short man, but strong and agile.
I was daring enough to lead
the bold expedition that named
this entire New World.

Amerigo Vespucci was just a merchant
on one of my ships, and even though
the foolish mapmaker chose his name
instead of mine, the true honor
of claiming this vast wilderness
still rightfully belongs to me.

Someday, all maps and charts
will proclaim the Alonsos,
not the Americas!

Quebrado

The ship groans,
wind shrieks,
and I feel the storm
breathing
all around me
like an enormous
creature
in a nightmare
where beasts
growl
and chase. . . .

On a ship
there is no place
to run away.

Bernardino de Talavera

I am not a man of prayer,
but every hurricane earns its name
by falling on the feast day
of a saint who has the power
to calm wild winds
and spare fragile ships,
so even though I have no calendar,
and I am just guessing at today's date,
I roar the name of Santiago,
patron of my homeland,
Spain's armored warrior-saint,
galloping on his ghostly
white stallion
of clouds. . . .

Quebrado

Brigantines are slow ships,
sailing no more than five knots,
a mere crawl in the face
of hurricane winds.

The foremast is square-rigged
and massive like a thundercloud,
and the aft mast is rounded
like a graceful bird's wing,
but the pirate is not a real captain.
He's merely a failed farmer,
unable to steer accurately
in such a fierce gale.

Sailors cry out for help
from the only skilled mariner
on this vessel—the hostage.

Should we free him?
Can he save us?

Quebrado

The sky is a fiery waterfall.
Rain and lightning pummel the deck
from above, while giant waves
hurl us from side to side,
and fierce currents tug
from below.

Every force of nature grasps
at shards of worm-eaten
ship's wood.

While sailors call out
in anguish,
I cling to the rail,
expecting
to die.

Bernardino de Talavera

A good sailor should be able to smell
the spice of land while a ship is still far
from shore, so I sniff the wild air,
hoping for ginger, vanilla, and orchids,
but all I inhale is sulfur—lightning—
the storm dragon's breath,
a zigzag flame.

There is no terror greater
than the danger of fire on a ship.
With sailors demanding that the hostage
be set free to help steer,
I relent.

Even the worst enemies
can seem like friends
when storm winds
unite us.

Quebrado

The iron key
feels like a wing
in my hand
as it floats down
toward shackles
to save the life
of a captive,
even though
I know he is
a killer
who would never
free me.

Alonso de Ojeda

Murky waters rise,
flooding the hold
so that I barely
escape.

I used to be powerful,
but now I am useless,
so weak that I have to lean
on the slave boy's
bony shoulder.

I limp up the ladder,
out of watery darkness,
into a fiery storm.

Quebrado

Burning masts
plummet and crash,
shattering the deck.

Shredded sails
and tangled ropes
form a swaying web
of smoky nooses,
choking me,
seizing my breath.

Sailors screech
like demons,
then leap
and sink.

I throw myself
overboard,
onto a frothy wave,
hoping. . . .

Quebrado

Water
is heavy
and monstrous.

I writhe up
toward air,
gasping and gulping
as the ship's
last remnants
vanish. . . .

All around me,
men grasp and pull,
dragging each other
under.

Part Two

Brave Earth

Quebrado

Trapped on surging waves,
I struggle to swim in rain
that feels like spears
of shattered glass.

The ship is gone,
her tree-spirits rising,
transformed into air.

It would be so easy to give up
and just let myself sink,
but as soon as I begin to wonder
if drowning would be peaceful,
a sea turtle glides toward me
like a creature in a dream. . . .

The turtle is real, with a sucker fish
clamped onto its slick green shell,
and a forest vine tied to the tail
of the wriggling fish.

Out of the downpour,
a canoe appears as if by magic,
rowed by a man with long black hair.
He tugs at the slithery green vine,
leading the huge turtle
toward his boat.

He shouts, and even though
his voice is swallowed
by howling wind
and booming waves,
I understand that the fisherman
is telling me to reach for the turtle,
so I grab the rim of the shell,
and I clamber up,
pulling myself onto
the great beast
as it skims
the rough surface,
soaring toward safety. . . .

Naridó

The waves are mountainous,
but there is a spirit-boy
between peaks,
so I help him escape
on a turtle I caught
with my bring-it-back fish.

I pull the storm-boy
toward a sandy beach,
and when he cries out
with gratitude,
his odd words
sound like echoes
of my own
human tongue.

Quebrado

Feeling lost
in a whirl
of wind,
I breathe
and discover
that I am alive
with my feet
on firm land
and my heart
astounded.

Bernardino de Talavera

My ship, my crew,
the promise of a long
profitable life
at sea.

All are gone.
Only this struggle
to swim
remains.

Alonso de Ojeda

My poisoned leg
makes swimming impossible,
so I cling to a splintered board
and hope that somehow
it will carry me
to dry land.

I have survived
other shipwrecks
on perilous shores,
but I was strong then
and now I am helpless,
just an old man
surrounded
by devious phantoms
who try to steal
my makeshift raft.

Quebrado

The turtle hunter leads me
through the ragged ruins
of a flooded village,
and then uphill
along the edge of a forest
where the wind
uproots towering trees
and sends them
flying. . . .

We stop and crouch.
We enter a cave.

I expect darkness and silence,
but the torch-lit cavern
is filled with people, birds, dogs,
and music, a chanted story,
a heroic song.

Naridó

My world is safe in the leaping light
of palm-frond torches that surround
a circle of dancers.

Hollow-gourd rattles, bird-bone flutes,
tree-trunk drums with fire designs
painted on the sides.

Caucubú sees me and smiles.
Her name means "Brave Earth,"
and she is all that I know and love.

I take my place in the circle
of dancers, with the storm-boy
at my side, bringing his spirit world
into the cave, our only refuge
in this time of wind.

Quebrado

The enormous cavern glitters
with jagged crystals
and smooth ones.

The faces of the dancers
are painted with red zigzags
and black spheres.
My mother used to decorate me
in the same way, using *bija* seeds
and *jagua* fruit to ward away
stinging insects.

The women wear white cotton skirts,
but the men are almost naked.

Everyone stares at me
as if I am the one
who looks strange.

Quebrado

Safety.
Such a small word.

The cave bristles
with sharp crystals
shaped like beaks and claws,
and flowing ones that resemble
glassy waterfalls. . . .

If I am not dreaming,
then perhaps I am dead,
wandering along the paths
of an afterlife
filled with wildness
and beauty.

Caucubú

Naridó brings a boy
from another world, his arms and legs
encased in a skin of wrinkled cloth.

We stop dancing to laugh and wonder,
but we cannot pause long
or the Woman of Wind
and her beastly Huracán
will swoop down to crush us
with gusts of rage.

So we resume our rhythmic steps,
chanting about the ancient beings
who emerged from caves long ago.

Some turned into trees or birds,
while others became people—humans
who love to sing like birds
and dance like trees
in wild wind.

Naridó

Everyone calls me River Being
because I catch so many fish
with my feathered arrows
and winged spears.

Caucubú's father
is our leader, the *cacique*,
and her twin uncles
are the *behiques*,
magical healers whose cures
protect our village
from wind spirits
and water beings,
visitors from the worlds
of spinning clouds
and swaying fins.

Caucubú

When Naridó is close,
I feel like a storm
within a storm.

My father says I must marry
a powerful *cacique*,
but I love Naridó,
the best fisherman
in our village.

When Naridó is close,
my mind swoops
and tumbles
like the wind
in a stormy sky.

I am glad there is peace
at the center of each
hurricane.

Quebrado

Many years have passed
since I was small and whole
and free to dance.

Movement surges
up through my feet,
pounding
and rippling
like a whirlpool
in a stream,
round and round
until the story-song
flows to an end,
like a river
finally reaching
its deep heart,
the wide sea.

Caucubú

I wish the dance
could go on forever,
keeping me far
from the dread
of marriage
to a stranger.

Even my mother
expects me to accept
my father's wishes,
and marry someone
my father chooses,
instead of Naridó.

No one listens
to young girls
in love.

Quebrado

The hurricane
falls silent.

We step out of the cave,
and find masses
of writhing sea things
that look like snakes,
moons, flowers,
and stars. . . .

The Woman of Wind
taught all these creatures
how to fly.

What will the hurricane
teach me?

Part Three

Hidden

Quebrado

Villagers wade
through deep mud,
salvaging fragments
of their toppled homes.

All I find is a bell
like the one I rang
on the ship,
when I hoped to calm
the Woman of Wind
with music.

Calm winds were my hope
because I did not yet know
that a hurricane could free me.

Quebrado

I help Naridó weave new palm-frond roofs
beneath a sky of circling vultures
and shrieking parrots.

When children ask my name,
I cannot bear to speak the Taíno one
I knew when I was small and whole,
so I search my mind for a new name,
and while I search, the children decide
that I must have come from the air,
so they call me Hurará, "Born of Wind,"
even though I do not feel bold
and strong
like a hurricane.

I still think of myself
as a broken place, a drifting isle
with no home.

Bernardino de Talavera

Battered by reefs,
my hands are swollen,
scraped by the rough
coral stone.

Washed ashore like driftwood,
I am lost, and longing for sleep,
desperate for rest—but I need
to keep moving
until I find magic
or medicine
for my hands,
and hearty food,
and a big seagoing canoe
to carry me away
from this desolate shore
of shipwrecked hopes.

Alonso de Ojeda

This is my first true encounter
with weakness.

My leg is paralyzed
yet it aches and itches,
and drives me mad with fury.

After other shipwrecks,
there were bells, mirrors, and beads,
shiny trinkets of flotsam
to astonish the *naturales*.
This time, I find nothing at all
on the shell-littered beach,
nothing to trade
for food and potions.

All I have is my ghosts
and my fear.

Quebrado

Naridó's village is sheltered
by freshwater marshes
and wind-ravaged trees.

The thatched huts seem hidden,
but even on this peaceful shore
I cannot imagine ever feeling
truly safe.

The dark sea is huge,
and it brims with ships
that carry ferocious men
like the pirate
and Ojeda.

No matter how invisible
I feel, I will always be wrapped
in the memory
of life as a captive.

Quebrado

I give up my Spanish clothing,
and start to dress like Naridó,
wearing only a cotton loincloth
and a necklace of spiky
barracuda teeth.

The designs that Caucubú paints
on my cheeks and chin
soon begin to feel
like a protective covering,
even though they are really
just pictures
of fiery lightning
and radiant stars.

Caucubú

I venture just far enough inland,
to get away from the salty crust
left by hurricane waves.

I mound soft red mud into hills,
and dig holes with a sharp stick,
so I can plant spicy pepper seeds,
sweet potatoes, and corn.

Then I wait
for my world
to grow.

When I am a little older,
no one will be able
to keep me away
from love.

Quebrado

Many years have passed
since I was a child of the land
with my hands in moist soil.

Now, I am eager to plant yams,
peanuts, and papayas,
and pluck hollow gourds
from tangled vines
to make musical
maraca rattles.

I long to eat pineapples
that taste like golden sunlight,
instead of dry ship's bread,
and salted beef,
and sorrow.

Quebrado

I have discovered
a deepening fear
of the sea.

I stay away from Naridó
while he fishes, and I avoid Caucubú
as she leaps from rock to rock
at the edge of the tide,
gathering shellfish.

The water is no longer stormy,
but it holds memories
of bearded men
who capture tree-spirits,
and turn them into wooden ships
that serve as floating cages.

I have discovered
a deepening fear
of the past.

Naridó

I try to show the storm-boy
how to swim like a dolphin,
but his terror of water
will not let him listen.

So I work alone,
catching silvery marsh fish
in tapered baskets,
chasing swift river fish
into stone traps,
and wrapping the sea's
great gold-belly fish
in nets that fly out
over the waves
like wings.

The storm-boy is young.
He has not yet learned
that hope is stronger
than fear.

Quebrado

I explore farther and farther inland,
away from Naridó's futile efforts
to teach me courage.

Alone at midnight, I hunt
on the slopes of a mountain.
Naridó has warned me
that the whispering forest
is forbidden to villagers,
but I climb uphill anyway,
grabbing the slender trunks
of trembling saplings,
and shaking them
to make iguanas fall.

Then I roast the giant lizards,
listening as branches
whisper and sing
in a gentle breeze.

Caucubú

Each time my father speaks
of sending me away to marry
the *cacique* of another village,
I flee to a small hidden cave
where I huddle alone
in darkness, feeling certain
that bat dung and pale,
skittering, eyeless spiders
are more beautiful
than a life without love.

Naridó is the only one
who knows about this tiny cave,
a secret we have shared
since we were little.

As soon as he arrives
and we huddle together,
the darkness begins to feel
like home.

Quebrado

Storms follow me
wherever I go.

Once again,
the sky looks so heavy
that I would not
be surprised
if black clouds
sank to earth
and grew roots
in moist soil,
creating a wispy forest
of drifting air.

Mysteries follow me
wherever I go.

Bernardino de Talavera

I wander like a beggar,
never finding any living soul
to mend my wounds
and heal my hunger.

When I finally see a *natural*,
she is just a young girl
on a stormy beach,
watching the crash of waves
from another tempest.

Hidden by beach shrubs,
I wait for a chance to capture
the unsuspecting girl.

I could trade her for medicine,
or a canoe rowed by slaves. . . .

Alonso de Ojeda

The sight of the lone girl
infuriates me.

The phantoms of *naturales* destroyed my leg
and poisoned my mind
with troubling magic.

If I had my sword,
I would tame the girl
and her entire
ghostly tribe.

Naridó

I vow to fish so powerfully
that Caucubú's stubborn father
will let her marry me,
so I fish in a downpour,
guiding the tree-spirit
of my lively canoe
between snarling waves
that make the sea
look like a towering
mountain range
of water.

The Woman of Wind
and her beast Huracán
shriek and roar,
but I cannot understand
their furious, whistling,
wild language.

Caucubú

I wail and plead,
begging my mother
to tell my father
to send other fishermen
to rescue Naridó
from the hurricane,
but no one listens,
so I run away
from the lonely shore,
feeling monstrous.

Quebrado

The Woman of Wind
and her hurricane dragon
spin closer and closer.

I flee with all the villagers
to the same huge cavern
where we danced before.
Flutes moan, drums thunder,
and children weep.
Once again, we chant songs
of heroes and hope,
songs that make me wish
I could be heroic.

Instead, I stay hidden
inside the friendly cave,
dancing and chanting
while Naridó is alone,
lost at sea.

Caucubú

My father wears two dance masks,
one on his face and another
on his chest, as if he is trying
to divide himself
into sacred twins.

The shimmering masks
are made of manatee bones,
with glowing eyes—a blend
of gold, silver, and copper,
all the hues of sun, moon, and stars
swirled together like a marriage
of morning and midnight.

If unlike metals can merge,
why not people?

Naridó

Survival.
Huracán was not able
to drown me,
so I climb once again
toward the big
welcoming cave,
thanking all the near
and far spirits
for rolling waves
that carried
my canoe
back to shore.

Survival.
Some words
are even stronger
than wind.

Bernardino de Talavera

In the chaos of the storm
I lose track of the girl,
but I follow a fisherman
up to a vast cavern,
while Ojeda,
like a shadow
limps behind me.

The first thing I see
inside the cave
is the savagely
painted face
of the broken boy,
my servant.

Quebrado

Quebrado.
Broken.
The pirate's voice
booms a name
I had hoped to never
hear again.

He orders me to translate
demands for food, medicine,
and a big seagoing canoe,
but I refuse to speak.

I will not obey
bellowed commands
from a man
who still sees me
as his slave.

Part Four

The
Sphere
Court

Quebrado

Talavera's face is gaunt,
and Ojeda is stooped
like a helpless old man,
but all I see is coiled fists.

Villagers move toward them,
curious and friendly,
until I shout warnings.
I call the intruders monsters,
even though I know that both
the pirate and the conquistador
are human, and humans are capable
of living in unimaginably
monstrous ways.

Quebrado

All faces turn toward me,
both the painted ones
and the bearded.

I am the only one in this cave
who understands
two languages.

My quiet voice feels
like a small canoe
gliding back and forth
between worlds
made of words.

Caucubú

The unnatural beings
have hairy faces, and they stink,
so I cover my nose
while the storm-boy speaks
to my father and my uncles
about distant places
and danger.

He tells of a faraway land
where men wear skins of metal
and move swiftly atop creatures
that make them resemble
two-headed giants
with long wavy tails
and four legs that end in feet
as hard as stone.

He speaks of enormous oceans
crossed in *canoas* as big as islands.

He tells of mournful tree-spirits
trapped within the wood
of the huge boats.

The boats turn into cages
that capture the lives
of ordinary children
and force them
to float far away
from their island
homes.

Naridó

The storm-boy's tale
makes him frown and groan,
even when he tells of wonders—
a village woman in love
with a peaceful stranger
on a four-legged spirit
made of strength
and speed.

He describes his own
childhood as a marvel,
with songs learned
by listening
to chanted stories
told by birds.

Quebrado

Revealing my life's tale
is such a challenge
that, in order to keep myself
from weeping like a small child,
I begin to add sweet memories
of my mother's talking macaws
and my father's leaping horse,
and while I sing in Taíno,
the pirate glares at me,
and Ojeda stares,
his gaze a blank puzzle
of sadness or fury.

When I speak of my parents,
the words make me feel
less alone.

Bernardino de Talavera

All my years in the Americas
have passed without any need
to learn a tribal tongue.

There were always enough
quebrado children, divided souls
who found it easy to translate.

Now, my fate rests in the voice
of a broken boy who hates me.
He has grown bold enough
to defy me, but I can easily
make him timid again.

I know how to turn
newfound courage
into terror.

Alonso de Ojeda

Anger seeps
into my deep well
of fear.

In Venezuela,
I was the ruler of all
and now I rule nothing,
not even my own rotting leg
or the ghosts
or my fear.

So I wait for an end
to the broken boy's
confusing speech
in a language that sounds
like the familiar whispers
of hateful phantoms.

Bernardino de Talavera

Warriors with spears,
arrows, and war clubs
surround us.

Some wear masks
with glinting eyes,
and even though the metal
is not pure, I recognize
streaks of gold.

All I need now
is the broken boy's
clever voice
to help me befriend
this rich tribe.

Alonso de Ojeda

I would give up all my old dreams
of finding cinnamon, pearls, and gold,
if only I could learn to speak
the *natural* language,
so that I could beg healers
to cure my leg.

I would even give up
all hope of gaining
marvelous wealth
by selling the islanders
as curiosities
at market fairs
in Sevilla.

Caucubú

The storm-boy's tale
whirls through my mind
like a hurricane
in a nightmare.

When the noise of the storm
beyond our sheltering cavern
finally fades to utter silence,
my father proudly announces
that we will now descend
to the sphere court,
where skillful men
will play a ball game
to determine the path
of our future.

Quebrado

Sphere games
are an island's courtroom.

Playing ball helps leaders
turn their anger into energy,
so they can make wise decisions
about matters of warfare
and peace.

As a small child,
I used to play for fun,
but now I am old enough
to join the solemn team
who will decide what to do
about my tale of cage-ships
and slave traders,
the improbable story
of my true life.

Quebrado

The sphere of sap and cotton
is as hard as a tree, but it moves
as lightly as air.

Wooden belts protect our bellies.
We are not allowed to hit the sphere
with feet or hands, only our heads,
hips, shoulders, and knees.

I leap to strike with my forehead,
and in that instant of motion,
all worries vanish.
I fly. . . .
I soar. . . .

The sphere
looks like
a golden sun
guiding me up
into blue sky
where my mind
suddenly feels

completely clear,
even though
the future
is still cloudy
and uncertain.

Alonso de Ojeda

On the mainland,
trials by sphere game
are often said to end
with execution,
but I have no idea what to expect
on this bewildering isle
of troubling surprises,
so I stare at the healers,
hoping to make them
tremble
by revealing
my own terror.

If they see that I am
inhabited by native ghosts,
surely they will share
my fear.

Quebrado

The line between
captives and captors
flows back and forth
like high tide.

When I see such deep terror
in the eyes of Ojeda,
I remember how recently
he was the pirate's hostage,
and I was the pirate's slave.

Now, the only captives
are the same two men
who lived by preying
on others.

Caucubú

It must be the way
I watched Naridó as he ran
and jumped, guiding the sphere
from goal to goal.

My father noticed.
He decided.
I had assumed that the only verdict
to grow out of this ball game
would be punishment
for the two monster-men
who tormented the storm-boy,
but another announcement
quickly follows.

I will be sent away in the morning
to become the wife of a stranger.

I will be sent far away
from Naridó.

Naridó

I search for her face
in the raucous crowd,
but she is gone.

We will never laugh
together again,
unless I find her quickly,
and we run away,
leaving our village
and our families
forever.

Quebrado

I watch with joy
as tribesmen with spears
chase the pirate and Ojeda
toward an eastern swamp
where crocodiles lunge
and writhe.

Banishment.
Mercy.
My enemies
will be outcasts, not corpses,
but even if they were executed,
their deaths would not help me
to be any more free
and hopeful
than I feel
at this moment
of stunned relief.

Bernardino de Talavera

This green-water torment
is endless and murky.
We will probably starve
in the swamps,
or shrivel with fever,
or be torn apart by claws
and fangs.

Whatever tale
the boy told in his own
broken language
has worked like a testimony
in a courthouse,
condemning us
to danger.

At least we have a small
merciful chance
of survival.

Caucubú

My world
was once
so wide
and bright.
Now
it is narrow
and dark
as I crouch
alone
in this upside-down
realm of bats.

Only love and hope remain,
but they are enough
to help me smile
as I wait
for Naridó.

Part Five

The Sky Horse

Quebrado

First by sunlight
and later by starlight,
the whole village searches
for Caucubú and Naridó,
but their footprints
show that love
has carried them up
to a forbidden region
of misty forests
where only healers
are allowed to venture,
and not even
the hunting dogs
seem brave.

Quebrado

Villagers blame me for all
that has happened.

Children call me
a creature of magic.

The healers accuse me
of knowing secrets.

Caucubú's father
sends me away.

The village that once
seemed so friendly
will no longer be
my refuge.

Quebrado

Alone and roaming
through valleys and over ridges,
I sense my father's restlessness
stirring within me.

I am an outcast now,
but wandering almost feels
like going home.

There are no people
in this forest—no huts or fields,
just trees the height of clouds,
mossy branches that whisper
and sing in the breeze,
and spidery orchids
that dangle
like fingers,
reaching. . . .

Quebrado

Forests are sacred.
My father once told me
that he'd abandoned the army
because killing made him
heartsick, and acts of mercy
were his only chance
to understand heaven.
I was too young to know
what he meant, so my mother
led me into a thicket of trees
where I heard songbirds,
tree frogs, and cicadas.

I heard stillness too,
silent roots growing
and fruit ripening.

It was the music
of a distant spirit
growing closer.

Quebrado

As I search for Naridó and Caucubú,
I hear the rustling leaves
of a red-barked mahogany tree.
It sounds like a whispered plea
for freedom from a rooted existence.

Naridó fled the village without his canoe,
so when I find him, I will show him
this spirit-tree, and we will build a boat.

It will take a month to chop the trunk
with stone axes, and another month
to hollow it with bone scrapers
and smoldering leaves.

We will have to start beneath
a new moon, when sap runs slowly
and insects will not devour
the moist wood.

By the time the heavy trunk
is transformed into a light,

floating thing, Naridó will know
all the winding paths of streams
in this mountaintop haven,
and he will be able to fish again.

I will help him build a village,
and I will find a girl to marry,
and together, we will plant fields
and be farmers, letting our minds
grow rooted and leafy. . . .

We will create
our own peaceful
New World.

Bernardino de Talavera

I battle Ojeda for scraps
of swamp food—raw frogs
and the dank eggs
of stilt-legged marsh birds.

I even swallow the mosquitoes
that pierce my skin to steal my blood.

Ojeda hates me, and I detest him,
but it takes two men to wrestle
a hungry crocodile.

By the end of the first night,
we have saved whatever is left
of each other's miserable lives.

Quebrado

In a silky green meadow,
between stands of ebony and cedar,
I notice a movement,
and then a mystery—something huge
and four-legged, on this isle
where no tales are ever told
of large animals—no panthers
or tapirs, no cattle or goats.

I aim a makeshift spear,
only to discover that the beast
is just a horse, a blue roan mare
with a wavy tail and rippled mane.

Moving closer, I see that her color
is black and white hairs
so finely mixed
that they look smoky blue,
like a shimmering cloud.

Quebrado

The mare is tame.
I stroke her soft muzzle
and puff my breath
into her nostrils,
inviting her to memorize
my human scent
so that she will accept me
as a trusted companion,
a member of the herd.

After so much solitude,
the friendship of a horse
feels like a mysterious gift
from distant spirits,
so I call her Turey.
I call her "Sky."

Quebrado

Turey and the green meadow
are so far from the swamps
that I should feel completely safe,
but questions begin to pound
through my nervous mind.
Is the horse alone, or did she escape
from an army of mounted invaders?

Are there explorers nearby,
searching for gold
and slaves?

Perhaps Turey belongs
to a lone wanderer
like my father.

If he is still alive and roaming,
would we recognize each other
after so many lonely years?

Quebrado

The mare is expertly trained,
an eager mount whose steadiness
reminds me how to guide a horse
with my voice, my legs, my hopes. . . .

I have no saddle or bridle,
no halter or lead rope. . . .

Clambering up the towering masts
of rolling ships must have helped me
preserve the art of balance.

I ride, I fall, I climb back up
and ride again. . . .

I feel like a giant,
gazing down at my world
from the height
of sky.

Quebrado

Alone in the meadow,
I practice all the cavalry skills
my father taught me
when I was little
and whole.

Sing to soothe your horse
when you are afraid.

Do not look down at the ground
or you will end up there.

Throw your heart over the fence
and your horse
will follow.

Bernardino de Talavera

After long nights of sleeping
in the branches of swamp trees,
and even longer days
spent searching
for any sign
of solid ground,
I find myself
absurdly grateful
for any company at all,
even though Ojeda
begins to sound
more and more
like a madman,
with his endless,
rambling speeches
about swords
and ghosts.

Alonso de Ojeda

Talavera still thinks of me
as his helpless captive,
but once I conquer
these phantoms,
they will be glad to fight
at my side,
instead of battling
within me
and against me.

The pirate will soon
find himself
outnumbered.

Caucubú

While Naridó tries to catch
a few river fish for dinner,
I squeeze the bitter juice
from wild manioc tubers,
so that we can eat
toasted cassava bread
and live like humans
in our wild little village
of two.

We are happy together,
yet lonely also,
aware of distance
and time.

Our families are so far away,
and the sea of days we knew
when we were younger
has grown tangled with chores
and exhaustion.

Narido

Without a canoe,
I have lost my rough power.
I lack the magic of swiftness,
the ability to glide toward fish
that can never swim fast enough
to escape.

So I sit by a stream, wondering
how we will survive on our own,
and then I see him, the storm-boy,
my born-of-wind friend.

He races on towering legs.
He has grown two-headed,
with a feathery crest and flowing tail.

He seems to fly—he must be
part bird or part spirit.

Quebrado

Turey is the one who finds them
with her sensitive nose
and swiveling ears.

I leap off her back,
to help my friends understand
that I have not changed.

At first, Caucubú looks frightened,
but Naridó reminds her that my father
rode a marvelous four-legged beast
in the tale I chanted when the pirate
first appeared in the cave of dancers.

Caucubú smiles and agrees
that hurricane songs are often filled
with impossible dreams
that turn out to be real.

Caucubú

The storm-boy and his sky beast
make the forest seem even more
remote and eerie than before,
but a little less lonely too,
and more exciting.

He teaches us how to ride Turey,
and she carries all three of us
on her sturdy back to a red tree
that resembles
an upright canoe.

Yearning fills Naridó's eyes
as soon as he sees the tree
and hears the leaves whisper.
He is eager to carve a new boat,
to keep our hopes
from sinking.

Quebrado

I long to stay hidden forever,
carving boats and dreaming
of safety.

On clear nights,
I climb to the highest branch
of the tallest tree.

I perch like a hawk,
close to the pictures
made by stars.

The glittering shapes
of mermaids and centaurs
help me imagine
distant life.

Quebrado

Imagining
turns into a circle
of possibilities
that leap and spin
in my mind.

Are there villages
beyond the eastern swamp?

What if the pirate and Ojeda
survived?

Would a song-story hero
race to warn the people
who live in that land
of far light?

I have a horse.
I can fly. . . .

Part Six

Far Light

Bernardino de Talavera

When we are hovering
on the very edge of starvation,
natural warriors appear
like spear-bearing angels.

They lead us
out of the swamp
and into their heaven
of thatched huts.

We are joyful with feasting
and magical cures.

Alonso de Ojeda

The coral cuts on Talavera's hands
are quickly mended, and even
my poisoned leg is healing.

Each evening, we sit around
the *barbacoa* fire, where natives
offer us our fill of lobster, shark,
and crocodile.

I still wear my armor
and my amulet, along with fangs
and claws from all the beasts
I have swallowed.

Soon, I will seize a canoe
from this generous tribe,
and the ghosts will serve
as my oarsmen. . . .

Quebrado

Balanced on Turey's back,
I creep through forests
and canter across grasslands,
skirting swamps until I finally reach
an open coast
of leaping waves
and twirling dolphins.

As I gallop
along sandy beaches,
the land, sea, and air
feel like one.

My fear of the shore
has been transformed
into exhilaration.

No one can capture
and cage
a horseman.

Alonso de Ojeda

Voices, vultures, faces, hands . . .
and now an avenging phantom
galloping toward me . . .

All the ghosts are happy to see
this mounted specter.
They must know that he will speak
in their language of sighs,
revealing my past to the village,
announcing that I am a killer
of chieftains.

So I rush, I charge, I clasp
the horseback phantom's
narrow wrist.

He twirls away
from my weakened grip,
and when he glances
into my eyes,

I see that he is real,
just the broken boy
from the pirate's
storm-swallowed ship.

Without my sword,
all I have is a sliver of shell
from the beach,
so I struggle
to use its sharp edge
as a knife blade,
to slice away
the boy's
defiant fingers.

Without hands,
he will never be able to hold
reins to guide horses
meant for knights. . . .

Bernardino de Talavera

I yank Ojeda away from the boy,
but it is too late to stop
this disaster.

Warriors surround me,
even though the boy is unharmed,
his hand intact.

Ojeda's rough madness
has turned our rescuers
into attackers.

With spears at my throat
I remain silent, hoping to evade
any appearance of sharing
the madman's
useless rage.

Quebrado

Villagers subdue both men
at spear point, while I canter
wide circles
around the edge
of chaos.

I never imagined that the pirate
would try to protect me,
not even in a futile attempt
to protect himself.

All around me,
there is turmoil.

No one in this village
has ever seen any creature
the size of a horse.

Alonso de Ojeda

The boy displays a mounted dance
of horseback leaps and pirouettes
that convince me he is a master
of spells.

If I ever reach any Spanish town,
I will see this strange boy
and all my other
natural phantoms
burned at the stake.

I will see Talavera
hanged by the neck.

I will see my own name
on every proud map
of impossible islands
and perilous continents.

Bernardino de Talavera

The prancing mare
and the broken boy's
two languages
must seem like magic
to the chieftain
and the healers.

While Ojeda and I
are held prisoner,
the boy is free
to tell the same tale
that condemned us
once before.

This time, I fear
his words might kill us.

Quebrado

After dancing and sphere games,
the village *cacique* is willing
to execute my enemies,
or banish them forever.
The choice is mine.

Heroes in songs make easy decisions.
They kill without conscience,
but in real life, deciding is torment.
I think of my father at the moment
when he resolved to leave the army.
I remember my mother's people,
who settled disputes by trading names,
a peace pact that turned rivals into friends,
offering everyone a fresh start.

I think of the quiet times
between hurricanes.
I dream of the peace
in a forest.

Bernardino de Talavera

We row away from the island,
arguing about who will be captain.

I imagine Ojeda thinks
he has captured the whole world
in this tiny canoe,
but we are alone
in our exile.

We have nothing left
but oars and the sea,
endless distance . . .
endless time. . . .

Yacuyo

As soon as I am alone
on a sunlit beach,
I shed all my old names,
both the gentle ones
given by my parents,
and the rough names
I received from my life
as a ship's slave
in hurricane season.

I choose the name
of a place—Yacuyo,
"Far Light."

The name glows brightly.
It carries me galloping
on my sky horse
all the way back
to the sheltering forests
of high mountains

where I have friends
and a home.

I no longer feel
like Quebrado,
a broken place,
half floating isle
and half
wandering wind.

I am free
of all those old
shattered ways
of seeing myself.

I am whole.

AUTHOR'S NOTE

I became fascinated by the first Caribbean pirate shipwreck while researching my own family history. One of my ancestors was a Cuban pirate who used his treasure to buy the cattle ranch where many generations of my mother's family were born. It was a ranch I loved visiting when I was a child. I especially loved riding horses.

The 1511 Spanish conquest of Cuba came so close to genocide that most historians regard Cuban Indians as extinct.

While researching this story, I learned that throughout the sixteenth and seventeenth centuries, the region around my ancestors' ranch was known as *un pueblo indio*, "an Indian community." I became a subject of the Cuban DNA Project, and discovered that I carry a genetic marker verifying tens of thousands of years of maternal Amerindian ancestry.

I am a descendant of countless generations of women like Caucubú. Indigenous Cubans do survive in body, as well as spirit.

HISTORICAL NOTE

Characters and Events

This book is a fictional account of historical events that were variously recorded by early chroniclers as having taken place in 1509 or 1510. Quebrado is an invented character. The others are historical figures, but I have imagined numerous details.

During the Age of Exploration, an estimated one of every seven vessels that left Europe sank or was wrecked by storms.

In the early years of the Spanish conquest, horsemanship was forbidden to natives of the Americas, who were only allowed to ride donkeys. Indians who defied the ban became some of the world's finest horsemen. The speed offered by horses allowed some to reach mountain hideouts, where they had a chance of survival.

Bernardino de Talavera was an impoverished conquistador who had worked all the Indians on his land grant to death. To avoid debtors' prison, he stole a ship and became the first pirate of the Caribbean Sea.

Alonso de Ojeda (also spelled Hojeda) arrived in the New World on the second voyage of Columbus in 1493. Ojeda led the brutal conquest of Hispaniola, and became notorious for his cruelty. He was one of the first Europeans to capture Indians and sell them as slaves. He led an expedition to South America that included Amerigo Vespucci, for whom the Americas are named. As governor of Venezuela, Ojeda was wounded by a poisoned arrow. Desperate for help, he accepted a ride from Talavera, who took him prisoner. The pirate and his hostage were shipwrecked together off the south coast of Cuba. After encounters with Indians and an ordeal in the swamps, they reached Jamaica in a canoe. Talavera was hanged for piracy, and Ojeda settled in Santo Domingo. According to legend, Ojeda ended his days as a mad pauper who asked to be buried under the doorway of a monastery, so that all who entered would step on his bones.

Caucubú was the daughter of a Ciboney (also spelled Siboney) chieftain. When she fell in love with a fisherman called Naridó, her father disapproved. She hid in a cave to avoid an arranged marriage.

Some of the caves of Trinidad de Cuba are now

nightclubs for modern salsa dancers. In La Cueva Maravillosa (The Cave of Marvels) there is a fountain honoring Caucubú, who is said to grant wishes. People claim that on moonlit nights she can be seen near the mouth of the cavern, surrounded by fruit and flowers as she waits for Naridó.

Culture and Language

Cuba's Taíno and Ciboney Indians spoke closely related dialects, performed ceremonial round dances, and shared a belief in spirits of the forest, sea, and sky. Peace between neighboring tribal groups was maintained through diplomatic marriages, a ritual precursor of soccer, and name trading, a practice that gave enemies a fresh start.

Many English words have Taíno roots. Examples include *barbecue, barracuda, canoe, cassava, guava, hammock, hurricane, iguana, manatee, papaya, savannah,* and *tobacco.* Spanish words with Taíno origins include *ají* (chile pepper), *guacamayo* (macaw), *maíz* (corn), *maní* (peanuts), *maracas* (rattles), and *yuca* (manioc). Cuba's distinctive variety of Spanish is even more widely enriched by Taíno terms, such as *bohío* (thatched house), *cocuyo* (firefly), *guagua* (transportation), *guajiro* (farmer), *guateque* (feast), and *manigua* (jungle).

Columbus gave Cuba the Spanish name Juana. Later attempts to give the largest Caribbean island a colonial name included Fernandina, Santiago, and Ave María. Only the original Taíno name has survived into modern times. One speculative translation is *cu* (friend) combined with *ba* (big). Other indigenous place names include Bahamas, Borinquén (Puerto Rico), Guantánamo, Haiti, Havana, Jamaica, and Quisqueya (the Dominican Republic).

Literature

For five centuries, the love story of Caucubú and Naridó has been told and retold by Cuban authors, with various endings and different interpretations of the young couple's names. My translations of Caucubú as "Brave Earth," and Naridó as "River Being," are based on Taíno lexicons in modern references.

It is tempting to associate Brave Earth with the "brave new world" speech of Miranda in act 5, scene 1, of William Shakespeare's marvelous play *The Tempest*. Scholars have never been able to verify all the British

playwright's sources of inspiration. It is intriguing to imagine him in a smoky inn on a foggy night, listening to some wandering seafarer's tale of hurricanes, castaways, caves, masked dancers, island spirits, forbidden love, and a girl named Brave Earth.

REFERENCES

Arciniegas, Germán. *Caribbean Sea of the New World*. Translated by Harriet de Onís. New York: Alfred A. Knopf, 1954.

Horwitz, Tony. *A Voyage Long and Strange*. New York: Henry Holt and Co., 2008.

Keegan, William F., and Lisabeth A. Carlson. *Talking Taíno: Caribbean Natural History from a Native Perspective*. Tuscaloosa: The University of Alabama Press, 2008.

Las Casas, Bartolomé de. *Historia de las Indias*. Madrid: Alianza Editorial, 1957.

Pané, Fray Ramón. *An Account of the Antiquities of the Indians*. Durham: Duke University Press, 1999.

Rouse, Irving. *The Tainos: Rise and Decline of the People Who Greeted Columbus*. New Haven: Yale University Press, 1992.

Sauer, Carl Ortwin. *The Early Spanish Main*. Berkeley: University of California Press, 1966.

Tabio, Ernesto E., and Estrella Rey. *Prehistoria de Cuba*. La Habana: Editorial de Ciencias Sociales, 1985.

Wright, Irene Aloha. *The Early History of Cuba, 1492–1586*. New York: Macmillan, 1916.

ACKNOWLEDGMENTS

I thank God for the quiet times between storms.

As always, I am grateful to Curtis, Victor, Nicole, and the rest of my family.

Special thanks to Pamela S. Turner, Martha Moreira Yunis, the Cuban DNA Project, and the Museum of the American Indian, Smithsonian Institution.

For helping me rescue this manuscript from numerous shipwrecked drafts, I am profoundly grateful to my wonderful editor, Reka Simonsen. I am also deeply indebted to Tim Jones, Laura Godwin, Deirdre Jacobson, Rich Deas, Liz Herzog, Sarah Dotts Barley, and the entire Holt/Macmillan team.

Go Fish!

GOFISH

MARGARITA ENGLE

What did you want to be when you grew up?
I wanted to be a wild horse.

When did you realize you wanted to be a writer?
As a child, I wrote poetry. Stories came much later. I always loved to read, and I think that for me, longing to write was just the natural outgrowth of loving to read.

What's your first childhood memory?
When I was two, a monkey pulled my hair at the Havana Zoo. I remember my surprise quite vividly.

What's your most embarrassing childhood memory?
When I was very little, we lived in a forest. I wandered around a hunter's cabin, and found a loaded gun behind a door. I remember feeling so terribly ashamed when people yelled at me for pointing the gun at them. I had no idea I was doing anything wrong.

What's your favorite childhood memory?
Riding horses on my great-uncle's farm in Cuba.

As a young person, who did you look up to most?
Growing up in Los Angeles, I participated in civil rights marches. I admired Martin Luther King Jr. I was also a great fan of Margaret Mead. I wanted to travel all over the world, and understand the differences and similarities between various cultures.

What was your worst subject in school?
Math and PE. I was a klutz in every sport, and I needed a tutor to get through seventh-grade algebra. In high school, my geometry teacher crumpled my homework, threw it on the floor, stepped on it, and said, "This is trash!"

What was your best subject in school?
English. I loved reading, and I loved writing term papers.

What was your first job?
Cleaning houses.

How did you celebrate publishing your first book?
Disbelief, and then scribbling some more.

Where do you write your books?
I do a lot of my writing outdoors, especially in nice weather.

Where do you find inspiration for your writing?
Old, dusty, moldy, tattered, insect-nibbled history books, and the stories my mother and grandmother used to tell me about our family.

Which of your characters is most like you?
I'm not nearly as brave as any of my characters.

SQUARE FISH

What in particular drew you to this history of the first Caribbean pirate shipwreck?
I am fascinated by moments when languages and ways of life meet. Even though history books said Cuban Indians were extinct, I felt certain that there must have been survivors. Little did I know that a DNA test would prove that I am a descendant of those survivors! (I am also a descendant of pirates. We can't choose our ancestors.)

What was the most difficult part of writing this story?
The voices of cruel people are a struggle. I don't like giving a mean person even one page of my attention, but the truth is that without many pages devoted to understanding them, those bad guys have more power, not less.

What kind of research did you have to do for *Hurricane Dancers*? Was there anything that you wished you could have included?
The research was incredibly challenging! That far back in time, very little was written. I had to depend on accounts by two priests. Fortunately, they were priests who defended the Indians, so they did not regard European conquerors as heroes.

I would have loved to include photographs of archaeological sites with cave paintings.

If you and Quebrado ever met, what would you like to say to him?
I would tell him that his people are not forgotten. They live on in my DNA, and in my imagination.

Hurricane Dancers is a Pura Belpré Honor Award winner. What was that experience like for you?
Every award I've ever received has come as a thrilling

surprise. I think of *Hurricane Dancer*'s Pura Belpré Honor, Américas Award, and International White Ravens Honor as belonging to the spirits of people who lived long ago and were forgotten by history. All I did was try to help readers imagine their lives.

What would you most like readers to remember from *Hurricane Dancers*?
I hope young people will remember the importance of peacekeeping traditions. I hope they can imagine trading names with someone from a different ethnic background. Maybe they will dream up their own peacemaking customs. What can we do to understand each other? What are our choices?

Are you a morning person or a night owl?
Morning. By noon, I am just a phantom of my morning self, and by evening, I turn into a sponge—all I can do is read, not write.

What's your idea of the best meal ever?
A Cuban guateque. It's a country feast on a farm. It comes with music, jokes, storytelling, and impromptu poetry recitals by weathered farmers with poetic souls.

Which do you like better: cats or dogs?
I love to walk, so definitely dogs. We always have at least one cat, but cats don't like to go places. Dogs are much more adventurous.

What do you value most in your friends?
Honesty and kindness.

Where do you go for peace and quiet?
A pecan grove behind our house at least twice a day, and the Sierra Nevada Mountains, at least twice a week. When I really need tranquility, I visit giant sequoia trees. Their size, age, and beauty help me replace anxieties with amazement.

What makes you laugh out loud?
Funny poems. The sillier, the better.

What's your favorite song?
I love the rhythms and melodies of old Cuban country music, but my favorite lyrics are from a reggae song by Johnny Nash, "I Can See Clearly Now."

Who is your favorite fictional character?
That changes constantly. In other words, the one I am reading about at the moment.

What are you most afraid of?
Tidal waves, nightmares, and insomnia.

What time of year do you like best?
Spring.

What's your favorite TV show?
So You Think You Can Dance.

If you were stranded on a desert island, who would you want for company?
My husband.

If you could travel in time, where would you go?
My grandmother's childhood.

What's the best advice you have ever received about writing?
Don't worry about getting published. Just write for yourself.

What would you do if you ever stopped writing?
Read.

What do you like best about yourself?
Hope.

What is your worst habit?
Self-criticism. Talking mean to myself. I can be very discouraging.

What do you consider to be your greatest accomplishment?
Finding the poetry in history.

Where in the world do you feel most at home?
Forests and libraries.

What do you wish you could do better?
Don't worry, be happy.

What would your readers be most surprised to learn about you?
My husband is a volunteer wilderness search-and-rescue dog trainer/handler. He and his dogs search for lost hikers in the Sierra Nevada Mountains. I hide in the forest during practice sessions. I am classified as a volunteer "victim."

SQUARE FISH

In the midst of the Cuban revolution, Rosa, a nurse, uses hidden caves as a haven for the sick and injured.

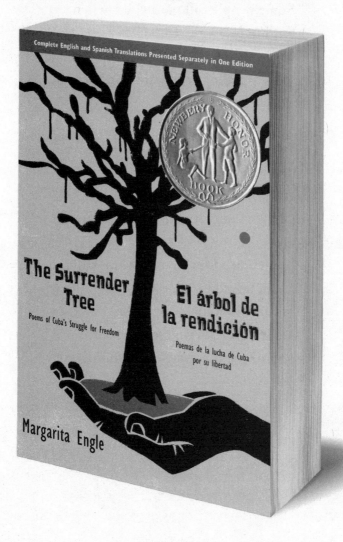

Can Rosa heal a country torn apart by war? Read about her in

The Surrender Tree

Rosa

Some people call me a child-witch,
but I'm just a girl who likes to watch
the hands of the women
as they gather wild herbs and flowers
to heal the sick.

I am learning the names of the cures
and how much to use,
and which part of the plant,
petal or stem, root, leaf, pollen, nectar.

Sometimes I feel like a bee making honey—
a bee, feared by all, even though the wild bees
of these mountains in Cuba
are stingless, harmless, the source
of nothing but sweet, golden food.

Rosa

We call them wolves,
but they're just wild dogs,
howling mournfully—
lonely runaways,
like *cimarrones*,
the runaway slaves who survive
in deep forest, in caves of sparkling crystal
hidden behind waterfalls,
and in secret villages
protected by magic

protected by words—
tales of guardian angels,
mermaids, witches,
giants, ghosts.

Rosa

When the slavehunter brings back
runaways he captures,
he receives seventeen silver *pesos*
per *cimarrón,*
unless the runaway is dead.
Four *pesos* is the price of an ear,
shown as proof that the runaway slave
died fighting, resisting capture.

The sick and injured
are brought to us, to the women,
for healing.

When a runaway is well again,
he will either choose to go back to work
in the coffee groves and sugarcane fields,
or run away again
secretly, silently, alone.

Lieutenant Death

My father keeps a diary.
It is required
by the Holy Brotherhood of Planters,
who hire him to catch runaway slaves.

I watch my father write the numbers
and nicknames of slaves he captures.
He does not know their real names.

When the girl-witch heals a wounded runaway,
the *cimarrón* is punished, and sent back to work.
Even then, many run away again,
or kill themselves.
But then my father chops each body
into four pieces, and locks each piece in a cage,
and hangs the four cages on four branches
of the same tree.

That way, my father tells me, the other slaves
will be afraid to kill themselves.
He says they believe
a chopped, caged spirit cannot fly away
to a better place.

Rosa

I love the sounds
of the jungle at night.

When the barracoon
where we sleep
has been locked,
I hear the music
of crickets, tree frogs, owls,
and the whir of wings
as night birds fly,
and the song of *un sinsonte*,
a Cuban mockingbird,
the magical creature
who knows how to sing
many songs all at once,
sad and happy,
captive and free . . .

songs that help me sleep
without nightmares,
without dreams.

Rosa

The names of the villages where runaways hide
are *Mira-Cielo*, Look-at-the-Sky
and *Silencio*, Silence
Soledad, Loneliness
La Bruja, The Witch. . . .

I watch the slavehunter as he writes his numbers,
while his son,
the boy we secretly call Lieutenant Death,
helps him make up big lies.

The slavehunter and his boy agree to exaggerate,
in order to make their work
sound more challenging,
so they will seem like heroes
who fight against armies with guns,
instead of just a few frightened, feverish, hungry,
escaped slaves,
armed only with wooden spears,
and secret hopes.

Lieutenant Death

When I call the little witch
a witch-girl, my father corrects me—
Just little witch is enough, he says, don't add girl,
or she'll think she's human, like us.

A pile of ears sits on the ground,
waiting to be counted.

This boy has a wound,
my father tells the witch.
Heal him.

The little witch stares at my arm, torn by wolves,
and I grin,
not because I have to be healed by a slave-witch,
but because it is comforting to know
that wild dogs
can be called wolves,
to make them sound
more dangerous,
making me seem
truly brave.

Rosa

The slavehunter and his son
both stay away during the rains,
which last six months, from May
through October.

In November he returns with his boy,
whose scars have faded.

This time they have their own pack of dogs,
huge ones,
taught to follow only the scent
of a barefoot track,
the scent of bare skin from a slave
who eats cornmeal and yams,

never the scent of a rich man on horseback,
after his huge meal of meat, fowl, fruit,
coffee, chocolate, and cream.

Lieutenant Death

We bring wanted posters from the cities,
with pictures drawn by artists,
pictures of men with filed teeth
and women with tribal scars,
new slaves
who somehow managed to run away
soon after escaping from ships
that landed secretly, at night,
on hidden beaches.

I look at the pictures
and wonder
how all these slaves
from faraway places
find their way
to this wilderness
of caves and cliffs,
wild mountains, green forest, little witches.